THE LEGEND OF THE AFRICAN
BAOBAB TREE

THE LEGEND OF THE AFRICAN

BAOBAB TREE

Written and illustrated by BOBBI DOOLEY HUNTER

Africa World Press, Inc.
P.O. Box 1892
Trenton, New Jersey 08607

Text and Illustrations
Copyright © 1995, Bobbi Dooley Hunter

First Printing, 1995

Library of Congress Cataloging-in-Publication Data

Hunter, Bobbi Dooley.
    The legend of the African bao-bab tree / written and illustrated
by Bobbi Dooley Hunter.
        p. cm.
    Summary: Tired of the complaints of a beautiful tree growing on
the African plains, the Great Spirit turns the tree upside-down so
that its branches look like roots growing toward the sky. Includes a
section with information about some African animals.
    ISBN 0-86543-421-2 -- ISBN 0-86543-422-0
    [1. Baobab--Fiction. 2. Trees--Fiction. 3. Africa--Fiction.]
I. Title.
PZ7.H91656Le 1995
[Fic]--dc20   95-10045
                                                    CIP
                                                     AC

Printed in Hong Kong by Norman Graphic Printing Co.Ltd.

Summary: This legend reminds us to be happy
and proud just being who we are.

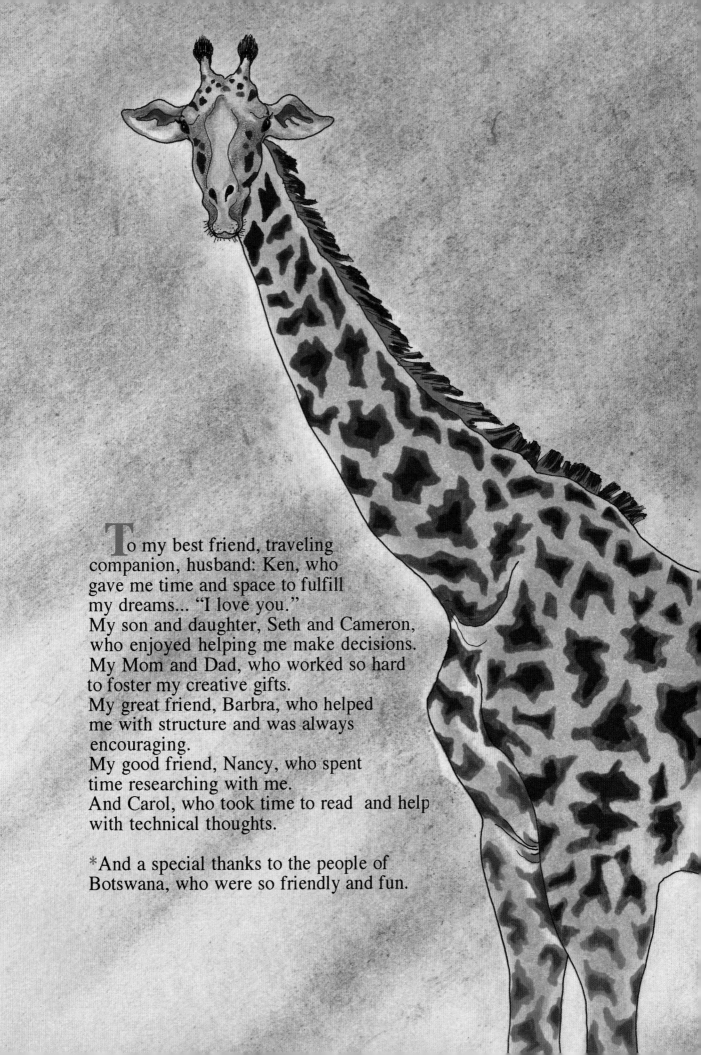

To my best friend, traveling
companion, husband: Ken, who
gave me time and space to fulfill
my dreams... "I love you."
My son and daughter, Seth and Cameron,
who enjoyed helping me make decisions.
My Mom and Dad, who worked so hard
to foster my creative gifts.
My great friend, Barbra, who helped
me with structure and was always
encouraging.
My good friend, Nancy, who spent
time researching with me.
And Carol, who took time to read and help
with technical thoughts.

*And a special thanks to the people of
Botswana, who were so friendly and fun.

Once there was a handsome green leafy African tree that shaded all the wild animals and people.

"**I** want to be the BEST and most HANDSOME of all the African Trees," he thought.

Each day he complained to the **GREAT SPIRIT of the WILD PLAINS**.

"**I** want to be the BEST, BIGGEST, BRIGHTEST, and most HANDSOME of all the African Trees," he grumbled to the **GREAT SPIRIT of the WILD PLAINS.**

One day the
GREAT SPIRIT of the
WILD PLAINS grew
annoyed. He reached
down and put his
mighty hand around the
large tree trunk. Even
the brave Wart Hogs
scattered.

The GREAT
SPIRIT of the WILD
PLAINS yanked the
tree out of the ground
in one raging, earth
shaking moment!

The GREAT SPIRIT of the WILD PLAINS heaved the green leafy African tree back into the earth UPSIDE DOWN! The rabbits hopped and hid in a hurry.

Suddenly the **GREAT SPIRIT of the WILD PLAINS** thundered, "I name you the BAO-BAB TREE," and the tree trembled and shook, because in Botswana, Africa, these words mean GIANT ROOTS!

To this day, the BAO-BAB TREE only grows green leaves once out of twelve months.

The other eleven months, the ROOTS bend and grow towards the GREAT SPIRIT of the WILD PLAINS.

A KEY
TO THE LEGEND
OF THE
BAO-BAB TREE

About the Tree

The *large* and *beautiful* **BAO-BAB TREE** grows in Eastern Africa. The branches, resembling roots, grow out of a thick trunk. The trunk, including the thick and thin branches, can grow 30 feet across and 200 feet high. The branches look like arms and fingers reaching towards the sky. The smooth trunk makes soft folds near the base just like an elephant's leg. Because of this, the **BAO-BAB TREE** is often called an Elephant Tree. In the spring, huge white flowers bloom developing into pear shaped dark fruit by summer.

A KEY
TO THE LEGEND OF THE BAO-BAB TREE

About the Animals

The Southeast African **Oryx Gazelle Antelope**, or Gemsbock, is found in the Kalahari Desert. They are a rowdy and tough animal with beautiful markings on the head, legs and flanks. They carry long, graceful horns and have large, floppy ears.

The most common **Zebra**, the Grants Plains Zebra, lives on open grasslands in Eastern Africa. They have wide, black stripes on their bodies. Narrow stripes run around their legs down to their strong, black hooves.

Cheetahs are the fastest animals in the African land. They roam the plains looking for game such as antelope, but they will also eat eggs and fruit.

The African **Giraffe** loves to eat tree leaves. With its long neck it can reach its food and see danger. Giraffes' spots are unique. Each Giraffe is born with its own "fingerprint" set of spots.

African **Ostriches**, the world's largest birds, stay in packs. With wings too small for flight, they run faster than any other birds. They use their strong legs and toes as weapons. People can ride on their backs if they can catch and harness them.

A KEY
TO THE LEGEND OF THE BAO-BAB TREE

About the Animals

The Great White Stork spends summers in Europe and winters in Southern Africa. They fly in flocks of thousands and eat locust insects. Some African people call them *the great locust birds*. Storks are endangered due to progress and the use of insecticides along with disappearing marsh lands.

The **Sable Antelope** * has unique facial markings. These large elegant animals are found in big herds in Eastern Africa. Sable means somber or dark. However, only the bulls are black. The horns of the Sable Antelope protect it against predators.

The **Wart Hogs** grow warts around their eyes to protect them while they feed on thorny bushes. They wallow in the evening and range on the plains by day. They use their long curved tusks as weapons or for lifting branches or moving rocks.

The Hedgehog, a small nocturnal rodent, nests in rocks and under brush. Its prickly, sharp spiny armor is like a pin cushion. The Hedgehog curls up into a ball for protection. It hunts for bugs, lizards, bees, birds and snakes along its bushy pathways.

Rabbits in Eastern Africa are called Bushman Hares and African Savanna Hares. Their gray and brown camouflage protects them from predators. Their short front legs and long hind legs make them strong runners and jumpers. They eat plants and live in colonies underground in long tunnels and large chambers.

A KEY
TO THE LEGEND OF THE BAO-BAB TREE

About the Animals

Elephants, the largest land mammals, have extremely huge ears and tusks. They use their trunks for eating plants, touching and feeling, and spraying themselves with dirt or water. They travel constantly in large herds to find new feeding grounds for their big appetites.

Lions, * lionesses and cubs of Africa are called a pride. The lion family has strong leg muscles for leaping, fine hearing and eyesight for capturing prey at night and their sharp teeth cut and tear meat from its bone. The male can weigh over 500 pounds. Other animals are wary when grazing near a pride.

The **Black Rhinoceros** and rare White Rhino are light and dark shades of gray. They live in central, eastern, and southern Africa. The horns of bone and hair on their face grow different lengths. They have very tough skin, yet they are sensitive to bug bites and sun. Even though they can weigh 1.8 tons, these shy animals are aggressive when frightened.

The Eagle is found everywhere in Africa. The most common, the Tawny Eagles, have the most varied diet. The African Fish Eagles love fish, but will eat any animal near the water. Eagles have a large wing span and huge talons or claws for grabbing their prey.

*Endangered species

A KEY
TO THE LEGEND OF THE BAO-BAB TREE

About the People

The African people live in Rondovals, which are round earthen adobe (mud and stick) huts with woven reed roofs. They grind their corn with large pestles in a carved hollowed tree trunk, often using parts of the Bao-Bab Tree. For musical instruments, they wrap hide around a hollowed trunk to make the sound of a drum. They use bone, ivory, wood or hands to make their sounds. For weapons, they carve long thin spears and knives. The people live off the land, only taking what they need. These friendly people live harmoniously with nature.

The
end